THIS LITTLE TIGER BOOK BELONGS TO:

_____

_____

_____

_____

For Mum and Dad
~ T.B.
For Chick and Babs
~ S.H.

LITTLE TIGER PRESS
An imprint of Magi Publications
22 Manchester Street, London W1M 5PG

This paperback edition published 1999
First published in Great Britain 1999

Text © 1999 Tony Bonning
Illustrations © 1999 Sally Hobson

Tony Bonning and Sally Hobson have asserted their rights
to be identified as the author and illustrator of this work
under the Copyright, Designs and Patents Act, 1988.

Printed in Belgium by Proost NV, Turnhout

ISBN 1 85430 600 6

1 3 5 7 9 10 8 6 4 2

THE GREAT GOAT CHASE

written by

Tony Bonning

illustrated by

Sally Hobson

Little Tiger Press

Mr Farmer had a field
and in this field he decided
to grow turnips.
So he ploughed the field and
sowed the seeds in long neat rows,
up and down, up and down,
until the whole field was done.

The seeds grew **and grew**
and soon every row was
filled with large, round,
plump turnips.

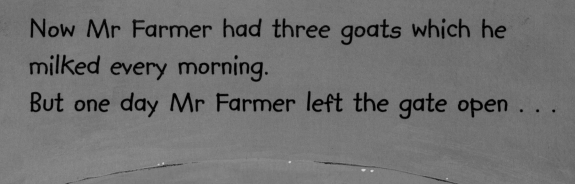

Now Mr Farmer had three goats which he milked every morning.
But one day Mr Farmer left the gate open . . .

. . . and the goats slipped through it, tripped
down the road and right into the turnip field.
They could hardly believe their good fortune.
Straightaway, they began to chomp the turnips,
row after row after row.

Mr Farmer, who was having a late morning cup of tea, looked out of his kitchen window and saw those goats gobbling up his turnips. "Oh no!" he wailed, running out of the door, spilling tea everywhere.

Mr Farmer then tried to chase the goats out of the field.
But those goats had minds of their own. One ran this way,
one ran that way and the third ran another.
Could Mr Farmer get those goats out of the turnip field?
No, he couldn't!

"I know," said Mr Farmer. "I'll get Dog."
He gave a loud whistle and Dog came running.
He rushed into the field and tried to herd the goats.
But Dog was a sheepdog and these were goats.
One went this way, one went that way and the third
went another, round and round the field until . . .

. . . Dog was exhausted.

Could Dog get those goats out of the turnip field?

No, he couldn't!

As Mr Farmer and Dog stood at the gate,
wondering what to do, Horse stuck his
head over the fence.
"What's the matter?" he asked.
"Are those silly goats too fast for you?"
"Probably," said Mr Farmer, wearily.
"Never mind, I've got good long legs,"
said Horse. "I'll soon have them
out of the turnip field."

Horse jumped the fence and raced up the field, sending turnips flying. Now Horse was bigger and faster than the goats, but they could turn more easily. One turned this way, and one turned that way and the third turned another way.

Could Horse get those
goats out of the turnip field?
No, he couldn't!

As Horse sat down beside Mr Farmer and Dog,
Cow came up to them.
"Let me show you how it's done," she said.
"My big horns will soon send them on their way."

And so they did.
One goat went scampering this way,
one goat went scampering that way
and the third went scampering another –
every way but the right way.
Could Cow get those goats out of the
turnip field?

No, she couldn't!

Now Pig, who had been grinning at the efforts of his friends, decided to show them how it was done.
"It's time to get tough," he said.
"Show them a bit
of muscle."

Pig pumped up his great shoulders and trotted into the
turnip field. Then he dropped his head and charged with
all his might. One goat nimbly tripped this way,
one goat nimbly tripped that way and the third
nimbly tripped another.

Could Pig frighten the goats out of the
turnip field?

No, he couldn't!

Mr Farmer, Dog, Horse, Cow and Pig all sat down
and cried their eyes out.
"**Boohoo, boohoo, boohoo,**" they howled.
Just then, Little Busy Bee came buzzing by.

"What's the matter?" she asked.
When they all told her, she said,
"I'll get those goats out of the
turnip field."
"You?" they exclaimed. "You?
A teeny weeny, tiny, winy,
totty wotty, wee wee bee?"
"Yes me!" she said.

Mr Farmer, Dog, Horse, Cow and Pig all stopped
crying and began laughing and laughing until
they were flat on their backs, legs-in-the-air
hysterical. When they had finished
splitting their sides, Little Busy Bee said,
"Can I go and get the goats out of the
turnip field now?"
"All right, off you go!" they said,
drying their eyes.

Little Busy Bee flew into the turnip field.
She buzzed round and round the goats'
heads, and then she said –

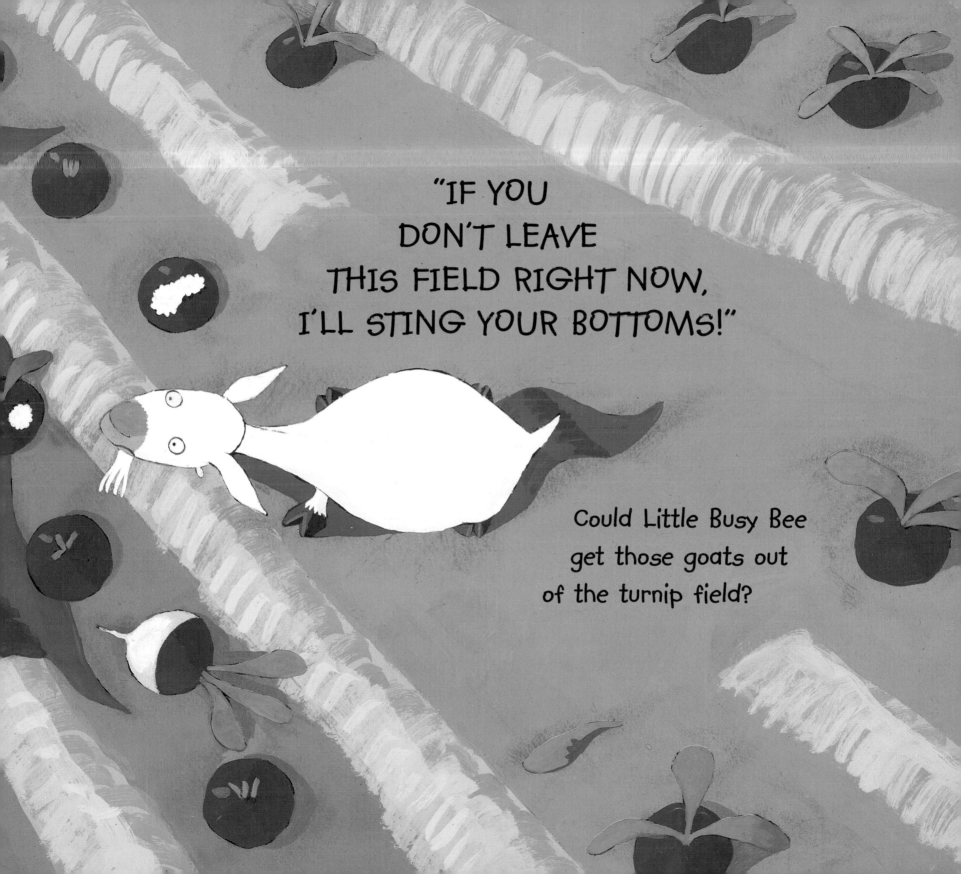

"IF YOU
DON'T LEAVE
THIS FIELD RIGHT NOW,
I'LL STING YOUR BOTTOMS!"

Could Little Busy Bee
get those goats out
of the turnip field?

YES, SHE COULD!

The goats didn't need a second
telling. As fast as their little hooves
could carry them they were off,
out of the gate, up the road
and on to the hillside.

At the gate Mr Farmer, Dog, Horse,
Cow and Pig all stood, feeling very silly.
"Sorry, Little Busy Bee," they said humbly.
And they all agreed that sometimes
little folk can do things much better
than big folk.

Join the LITTLE TIGER CLUB now for lots more books to enjoy!

Schools can join too and will receive a special enrolment pack.

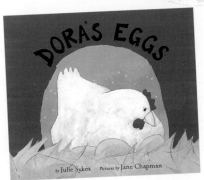

Join the LITTLE TIGER CLUB now and receive a special Little Tiger goody bag containing badges, pencils and more! Once you become a member you will receive details of special offers, competitions and news of new books. Why not write a book review? The best reviews received will be published on book covers or in the Little Tiger Press catalogue.

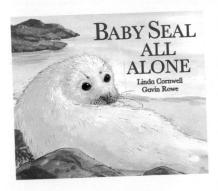

The LITTLE TIGER CLUB is free to join. Members can cancel their membership at any time, and are under no obligation to purchase any books. If you would like details of the Little Tiger Club or a catalogue of books please contact: Little Tiger Press, 22 Manchester Street, London W1M 5PG, UK. Telephone 0171 486 0925 Visit our website at: www.littletiger.okukbooks.com